The Magic Pumpkin

The Magic Pumpkin

By Bill Martin Jr.
and John Archambault

Illustrated by Robert J. Lee

Henry Holt and Company · New York

I walked into the garden
the afternoon of Halloween
to choose a jack-o'-lantern pumpkin
for this spooky night of in-between.

And there before me,
easily found
in a nest of leafy green,
lay a pear-shaped pumpkin,
indeed, a perfect pumpkin,
a royal prince of seed and vine,
just waiting to be mine.

As I reached for it,
that pumpkin—
it's hard to believe—
whispered in my ear,
perfectly clear,
"Choose me! Choose me
to be your guard!
I'll keep the foolies
from your yard!"

I was frightened,
but nonetheless,

with a knife well sharpened,
I gave the pumpkin
eyes and nose . . .

and grinning mouth,
which came to life
with candlelight,

to stay the mischief
of the night.

As I placed the jack-o'-lantern
at my door,
I think it winked
at the ghostly moon—
as if those two had preplanned
some tomfoolery
to happen soon.

And what was that?
An owl's cry
and a phantom wind

A moment later
twin foxes came
out of the wood
like hooded witches
and stood staring at me
with dreadful eyes.
I was stupefied.

Oh, no!
Through the hedge
now came
four mystic giants
disguised as skunks,
walking stiff-leggedly
across the yard
straight toward me.
I screamed for help!

blew my coattails
and did me in.
I fell speechless to the ground.

Mice came creeping
from their leafy runs
to mock me shamelessly
with their careless fun.

Suddenly
a band of foolies
came surging down the road,
banging, clanging,
boom-boomeranging,

tumbling wildly into my yard,
where my jack-o'-lantern pumpkin
was holding guard.

But that jack-o'-lantern pumpkin
was no longer mine!
His eyes glared!
His nostrils flared!

He sneered!
He snorted!
He danced!
He sang!

He was the leader
of the foolie gang!

I cried,
"You traitor!
Turncoat!
Double cross!
Tonight will be
your albatross!"

With that
I snuffed his candlelight . . .

and the turncoat withered
out of sight.

For David Canzoneri
and his patch of magic pumpkins

Henry Holt and Company, Inc.
Publishers since 1866
115 West 18th Street
New York, New York 10011

An Owlet Book and colophon are registered
trademarks of Henry Holt and Company, Inc.

Library of Congress Cataloging-in-Publication Data
Martin, Bill.
   The magic pumpkin / by Bill Martin Jr and John Archambault ;
illustrated by Robert J. Lee.
   Summary: A Halloween jack-o'-lantern leads a band of mischief
makers before getting snuffed out.
   [1. Jack-o'-lanterns—Fiction.   2. Halloween—Fiction.   3. Stories
in rhyme.]   I. Archambault, John.   II. Lee, Robert J., ill.   III. Title.
PZ8.3.M418Mag   1989   [E]—dc20   89-11162

ISBN 0-8050-1134-X (hardcover)
10   9   8   7   6
ISBN 0-8050-4904-5 (paperback)
10   9   8   7   6   5   4   3   2   1

First published in hardcover in 1989 by Henry Holt and Company, Inc.
First Owlet paperback edition, 1996

Printed in the United States of America on acid-free paper.∞